TOMORROW is a Chance to Start Over

BEDTIME STORY AND DREAM SONGS
BY HILARY GRIST

In a little red house in a city
by the sea, a brother and sister
were getting ready for sleep.

Mom read them a story
and kissed them goodnight.
She tucked in their covers
and turned out the light.

But the children couldn't sleep
no matter how hard they tried.
They could still hear the sounds
of the city outside.

Cars beeped and honked,
streets whirred and stirred.
"Don't they know it's bedtime?"
Ira wondered.

"Let's go somewhere quiet,"
Isabelle said.
So they got in a boat
and sailed off instead.

They floated away
from the bright city lights.
Away from the noises
and into the night.

Waves rose and
fell as miles drifted by,
lit by a lantern
and a moon-kissed sky.

At dawn, Ira held
a looking glass up to his eye.
"I see something in the distance!"
he happily cried.

A colourful island rose out of the sea.
Full of bright reds and yellows,
purples and greens.

A magical land
for them to explore.
So they landed the boat
and stepped onto the shore.

They followed a trail
that twisted and turned
to a bridge on a river
that bubbled and churned.

Leaves of all colours
drifted down the blue stream.
It was a beautiful sight
that seemed out of a dream.

The wind caught their wishes
and blew them away
over mountains and valleys,
dancing for days.

White clouds seemed
to wander off into the sky
while Ira and Isabelle
wished they could fly.

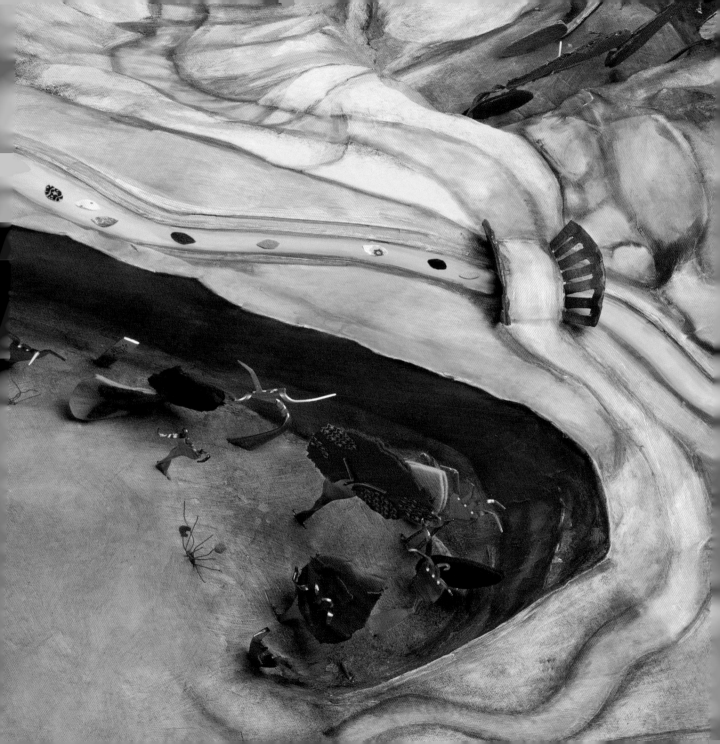

Up high a big robin softly sang down,
"Fly, fly, little ones!
Lift your feet off the ground!"

"On the count of three,"
both the children agreed.
So together they counted,
"One... Two...

Three!"

The pink sun was sinking
down low in the sky,
so the bird told the children,
"time to say goodbye."

"My dear little friends,
now that you know how to fly,
I must tell you something
to remember me by."

"At night while you sleep,
send your dreams out to sea.
The waves of the ocean
will bring them to me."

And lastly he left them with a special refrain, "Tomorrow is a chance to start over again."

Tomorrow is a Chance to Start Over

Lie down on your pillow
In the shadows
Close your eyes

Turn out the old lamplight
And sing goodnight
Lullabies

You are another day older
Soon you'll be through the dark
Tomorrow is a chance to start over
Start over again

Like the setting sun, dear
As it lingers
Falls to rust

I'll see you in my dreams, love
Let the long day
Turn to dust

You are another day older
Soon you'll be through the dark
Tomorrow is a chance to start over
Start over again

You are another day older
Soon you'll be through the dark
Tomorrow is a chance to start over
You'll re-ignite the spark
Tonight you can lie here on my shoulder
Soon you'll be through the dark
Tomorrow is a chance to start over
Start over again

Fall in My Loving Arms

Today is done
The last light has gone
Fall in my loving arms

The dark is long
Don't wait for the dawn
Fall in my loving arms

Let the moon spin around the sky
Let the world beg the sun to rise
Fall in my loving arms

The winds may howl
Outside in the storm
Fall in my loving arms

If rain pours down
We're here safe and warm
Fall in my loving arms

Let the moon spin around the sky
Let the world beg the sun to rise
Fall in my loving arms

Swallow
Me Up

Flooding through these veins
Miles and back again
Swallow me up
Swallow me up
Swallow me up
Safe under your tongue my love
My love

What is heaven for?
Just talk of distant shores
Swallow me up
Swallow me up
Swallow me up
Starting never stops my love
My love

Watching shadows fall
Underneath it all
Swallow me up
Swallow me up
Say I'm enough
And swallow me up
Say I'm enough
And swallow me up
Say I'm enough
Call this body home my love
My love

Float
Away

Like a leaf that drifts along the river
Float away
Like a leaf that drifts along the river
Float away

All through the night
I'll be holding you tight
'Til the first light warms your face

Like a seed that blows over the pasture
Float away
Like a seed that blows over the pasture
Float away

All through the night
I'll be holding you tight
'Til the first light warms your face

Like a cloud that wanders on forever
Float away
Like a cloud that wanders on forever
Float away

All through the night
I'll be holding you tight
'Til the first light warms your face

Like a cloud that wanders on forever
Float away

Le Petit Oiseau

Le petit oiseau qui chante
Pour vous mon cher amour

Le petit oiseau qui vole
Allez avec lui au ciel

Le petit oiseau qui rêve
Couche-toi sur les ailes ce soir

Say Goodnight

Say goodnight
Say goodnight

On go the waves to the shore
Hours as the dark spins outside our door
Send all your dreams out to sea
Wait as the tide comes to carry me

Safe in the palm of your hand
Ships setting sail for a distant land
Pull me in like gravity
Wild is the ocean that calls to me

City of Green and Blue

Look out the window
The shadows dance slow
Down into the machines
Streetlights so pretty
Veins of the city
Dreams made of concrete

Oh my city of green and blue
I'm coming back home to you
Oh my city of green and blue
I'm coming back home to you

Feels like forever
Since I smelled the salt air
All of my weight released
How long must I wait
Lying here awake
Tired eyes tired feet

Oh my city of green and blue
I'm coming back home to you
Oh my city of green and blue
I'm coming back home to you
Back home to you

I'll Be There

Let's stay up all night and count the stars
Underneath a fading light we'll compare scars
I'm starting to care
Oh no have I said too much?

I'll be there
Always there
I'll be there
Always there

Years I walked a crooked line now here you are
Right in front of my own eyes a mystery calls
Oh it's in your voice this knowing that is no choice

My dream's a lullaby holding your hand
A place without time
A song that never ends
You are my best
You are my best friend

Still

There's a part of me still
That won't turn off the light
'Cause monsters come at night
I run down every grassy hill
Jump over the cracks
Fall in love too fast

And though I'm older
My heart grows younger
Younger than yesterday
I'm wishing on a four-leaf clover
I will fly someday
Someday

There's a part of me still
That tries to catch a star
And wonders where you are
I know that magic isn't real
But something in your eyes
Something never dies

Story, lyrics, music and lead vocal HILARY GRIST

❀ Record producer MIKE SOUTHWORTH ❀ String arrangements MATTHEW ROGERS

❀ Story narration HILARY GRIST ❀ Recorded and mixed by MIKE SOUTHWORTH

at CREATIV RECORDING STUDIOS ❀ Mastered by HARRIS NEWMAN

MUSICIANS HILARY GRIST (piano, keyboards) ❀ MIKE SOUTHWORTH (bass, guitars,

percussion, background vocals) ❀ THE YALETOWN STRING ENSEMBLE and

STEFAN THORDARSON (cello, violin, viola)

Photography MIKE SOUTHWORTH and DAN JACKSON ❀ Set design ADAM THOMAS,

MIKE SOUTHWORTH and HILARY GRIST ❀ Clay character creation HILARY GRIST

❀ Set painting DANA IRVING ❀ Artistic director ROLAND STRINGER

❀ Graphic design STEPHAN LORTI for Haus Design

❀ Copy editor RUTH JOSEPH

HILARY GRIST and MIKE SOUTHWORTH would like to thank their loving families:

BOB, KAREN, KEITH, JOAN, RYAN, CHARMAINE, MAREYA, NYLA, MARTY, TRIN and LIVI.

Artist information available at www.hilarygrist.com

We acknowledge the financial support of the Government of Canada through the Department of Canadian Heritage
(Canada Music Fund) and of Canada's Private Radio Broadcasters.

Master recordings under license from Hilary Grist. All songs published by Hilary Grist

Ⓒ Ⓟ 2015 The Secret Mountain (Folle Avoine Productions)
ISBN 10: 2-924217-29-6 / ISBN 13: 978-2-924217-29-0
Ⓥ www.thesecretmountain.com